Tales of Sammy the Forester

by Martin John Faulkner

GREEN MAGIC

Green Magic
Seed Factory
Aller
Langport
Somerset
TA10 0QN
England
www.greenmagicpublishing.com

ISBN 978 1 739973322

Designed & typeset by Carrigboy, Wells, UK
www.carrigboy.co.uk

GREEN MAGIC

Contents

Chapter 1

Where is Sammy?

Sammy was a forester who lived many years ago in a small village, on a great moorland in the West of England. Imagine; that was a time when people travelled mostly by horse. They drank water from the springs and wells and told many a story around their winter fires.

Not too far away, across the moor, was a great wild wood that rose high above the marshland. So big was that wood, it would have taken a hedgehog a whole month to walk from one side to the other. So green and wild was the wood that the people of Bramley Village called it the leafy crown of Mother Nature. This was Bramley Wood; the place that Sammy, one of the seven foresters, loved so dearly and worked in all his life.

One fine morning in January, Sammy's son Gabriel was sitting on the arm of a wooden bench by the village green, waiting for Samantha, his friend. From the bench he could see along the street of stone cottages, past the church tower to the windmill on the hill beyond. While he was waiting, he looked up at the huge, majestic elm tree that towered high above him. There it stood with its long limbs in the blue sky, its strong roots deep in the earth and its great trunk silently sleeping in the cold winter air. All he could hear was the branches whispering to the wind, the animals out on the moor, and the river gushing over rocks in the distant Bramley Wood.

Just then, someone called his name from a nearby cottage. It was his mother, Isabel. She stood by the open door holding a brown cloth bag up in the air. "Look," she said, "your dad's gone to work without his lunch! It's a beautiful day, would you go to the wood and take it to him?" At that moment, Gabriel felt a tap on his shoulder. "I'll come with you!" A familiar voice said. It was Samantha. "Oh, alright," said Gabriel. "Would you like hot toast and jam first?" Called Isabel with a big smile. Then, before she could say 'ragged robin', they were both by the fire, ready with the toasting forks.

Soon they set off, feeling warm in their thick coats, down to the edge of the village and on to the muddy marsh track where the lapwings gather and the cotton grass dances in the wind. The further they walked, the more of Bramley Wood filled the sky, until they arrived at the old oak gate. Hanging on the gate post was a stout stick made of hawthorn. All shiny at one end was that stick. It had always been so that anyone who came to the wood should knock on the gate first to let Mother Nature know they were there. Gabriel held the shiny end and knocked on the gate three times. Just then, two deer sprang to their feet from the dried leaves and ran towards a far away holly thicket. It made the children jump! Shutting the gate behind them, they made their way along the gravel track toward the big stone bridge that crossed the River Mistle. The two friends stood on the bridge for a while and watched the swirling water oozing from the dark mouth of the river cave that lay deep

under the hazel wood on the hill. Then, up that hill they went, under the overhanging oak trees, until they saw the wooden cabin where the foresters met and the two grass paddocks where their horses grazed. The children noticed that there were no horses and the cabin door was shut. "The foresters are all out working somewhere in the wood," Gabriel said. "I wonder where Sammy is?" Sparrows were chattering in the hawthorn bushes and a big, grey wood pigeon was cooing on the roof. The children went into the cabin which was warm. It smelled of wood smoke and burnt toast. They cast their eyes around the walls. Each forester had his own special place to hang his tools. Gabriel noticed a gap where Sammy's best billhook cutter used to hang. "Ahh, my dad is sure to be somewhere in the west wood cutting hazel poles," said he. "Come on Samantha, let's go!" The two friends walked north towards the middle wood, and then took the track down to the great hazel wood on the western slopes. Soon they found fresh hoof and wheel prints in the mud. "I am sure this is the right way," said Samantha, placing her boots in the hoof marks. Then the prints suddenly turned sharply off the track and into the wood, vanishing in the deep layers of leaves. From now on they would have to guess…

After a while they came to a little stream, and who should be there swishing his tail, cheeks full of golden hay? It was Alder, Sammy's cream and brown dappled horse. Gabriel and Samantha ran up to Alder and hugged his warm neck. Alder always liked to be hugged. "Well, Sammy can't be far away now," Samantha said, peering all around the wood. "But where?!" Gabriel wondered. They walked a little further through the woodland where they saw many freshly cut hazel poles. They even

found Sammy's billhook cutter with its tip stuck in a rotten tree trunk. And there was Sammy's green and white spotted scarf, hanging on a holly branch. So where is he? They both called out: "Sammy! Sammy!" Just then, something bounced off Gabriel's hat, which landed in the dry leaves below. What was that?! They both looked among the leaves, but could only see twigs and hazelnut shells. Then, something bounced off Samantha's shoulder! They looked up in the overhanging branches expecting to see a squirrel. But there were no squirrels to be seen. That's strange, they both agreed. Then Samantha said in a whisper: "Look!" She was pointing to a huge oak tree nearby. There appeared to be steam coming out of the trunk. How could that be! Just then, Gabriel remembered that very tree. "Wait there," he whispered. He stooped down and took a handful of lovely dark leafmould from under the dry leaves. On tip-toes, he made his way to the old oak, pulled himself up on a branch and put his arm into a hole in the side of the tree. Sprinkling the leafmould through his fingers

Gabriel smiled cheekily at Samantha, who by now had got the giggles. Then came the loudest heartiest laughter from inside the tree! They both ran around it and on the other side was a big hole in the trunk. There was Sammy, inside the tree, with the morning sun shining on his face, a great big smile through his red beard and many lines of laughter around his deep blue eyes. There was leafmould all over his hat and shoulders. He opened his hand and there were nutshells that he had been flicking at them earlier. "Good morning you two," he said. "What a nice surprise to see you out here!" "You forgot your lunch," said Gabriel. "Yes, I know and the squirrels have eaten all the hazel nuts, so I may as well go and nibble hay with Alder," said Sammy with a chuckle. "Close your eyes Dad!" Then Gabriel placed the cloth bag in Sammy's lap. "You can open your eyes now!" said Gabriel. Sammy's face lit up like a dandelion. "Thanks Son!"

Sammy felt very glad later that day when he ate his lunch.
So did the ants as they ate the crumbs from around his boots.

Chapter 2

Martha

One winter morning in early February, the world was glistening with frost crystals, which glowed silver and purple in the rising sun. Sammy watched the pale moon setting behind the wood as he rode Alder across the marsh, wrapped tightly in his felt coat and hat. Alder puffed warm steam from his nostrils, his hard hooves crunching through the shallow sheets of glassy ice on the track to the wood.

As they passed through the forest gate, Sammy noticed how beautiful the frosty white branches looked against the blue sky. He could hear a squirrel cracking nuts somewhere in a nearby beech tree.

When Sammy arrived at the forest lodge, Jim the head forester was just drawing water from the well for the horses and the kettle. They greeted each other with cheery smiles and a "Good morning."

Then, on their way to the lodge door, they gently flicked a long row of icicles that hung from the roof. Perhaps they would make a tune!

That morning, Sammy rode west to the hazel wood to cut the first load of sticks for the hurdle fence maker. When they arrived, Alder found grass to eat beside a stream and Sammy stood for a while sharpening his billhook cutter. Then he noticed someone standing in a pool of misty sunshine there in the hazelgrove. Who might that be? He thought to himself. He put down his billhook cutter and began to walk a little closer. The person turned towards him.

Ahh, it was Martha! She wore a long green cloak and from under her hood there came a plat of hair that had once been as red as the fox. It was now laced with silver that flowed like a little stream down to her waist, tied at the end with woodbine and red hips of the field-rose. She looked at Sammy with her green eyes and put a finger to her lips: "Shhhh," she whispered to him as he stepped in the frosty leaves. "Look over there by the fallen tree…" When Sammy turned his head, he saw a baby deer limping badly. One of its back legs was hurt. Nearby was its mother, standing still and watching. Sammy knew that Martha wanted to catch the little deer. You see, she knew how to help hurt animals. It wasn't long before the two of them surrounded the little fawn. Then, carefully, Sammy lifted it from the ground. Sammy could feel its heart beating quickly in its warm little body through its soft brown coat. The baby deer looked at Sammy with its shiny frightened eyes as he carefully put it into Martha's arms. They rode down the bumpy track through a tunnel of bare hazel branches, the little deer safely cradled in Martha's lap at the back of the cart.

Soon they got to Martha's cottage deep in the woods. Her cottage stood in a clearing, its thatched roof white with frost on this cold February morning. Around the garden was a mossy stone wall with an old oak gate in it. Holly berries were glowing red in the morning light by the front door and a whisp of smoke rose from the stone chimney.

Sammy carried the young deer into the cottage and placed it in a willow basket that was padded with sprigs of heather. Martha put some

more wood on the fire and hung the kettle over it. "There," she said as she walked through a door into a room that was full of bottles and jars with every kind of herb, berry, flower, root, bark and stem that grew in Bramley Wood! Soon the kettle began to hiss. Sammy sat by the hearth and gazed around the room. It wasn't long before he noticed an overturned water jug on a shelf with a wood pigeon peering out over the rim. It had a broken wing. On the floor nearby was an old wooden fish box and in it was a fluffy red squirrel with both its back legs bandaged together. Then Sammy heard a whimpering sound down by his feet. He saw a little red fox curled up on a straw rug, mostly covered by Martha's old shawl. It had lost much of its fur.

Martha appeared carrying a heavy iron cooking pot in one hand and a wooden spoon in the other. She took the kettle off the fire and hung the pot in its place. The room soon smelled of cooking herbs and wood smoke. "Lovely cup of tea Martha," said Sammy. She smiled, busily stirring the herbs into a thick green paste. Martha then knelt down on the stone floor next to the little deer. "Please stroke its neck," she asked Sammy. She then took its back leg carefully in her hand and covered it with the warm green paste. Next, she wrapped it all up in a big leaf of butterbur and bound it with ivy stems. She held its leg with both hands for a while and whispered something to the deer that Sammy didn't understand. "There now," said Martha. She lifted the deer from the willow basket and handed it gently to Sammy. "Time to take our little friend back to the wood." Together they returned to the hazel wood. Sammy placed the young fawn on the crisp leaves and stroked its back. It looked around for a while and then hobbled out of sight.

Sammy still managed to fill the cart with hazel poles that day, as he did every day for the rest of the winter. But it wasn't until the first day in March, just before Sammy cut the last of the hazel, that he noticed something move nearby. It was a deer! A young deer jumping and leaping in and out of the hazel, and close by was its mother nibbling the first new shoots of spring grass. Sammy noticed a ring of ivy twine still around its back leg. The little deer stopped for a moment and looked at Sammy with its shiny brown eyes. It then followed its mother deep, deep into the hazel wood.

* * *

Sammy the Forester is cutting the hazel
And letting it fall to the ground.
Sammy is pleased with the hazel he is cutting
For the sticks they are long and round.

Soon he'll stop cutting and place all the sticks
In bundles of twenty-five.
Then he'll take out his twine and tie them all up
While he waits for the cart to arrive.

While Sammy is waiting he feels quite hungry
So, he sits with his back to a tree.
And in his cloth bag he has apples and oatcakes
And cobnuts twenty and three.

And now that he's eaten he stretches and yawns
And soon he falls fast asleep.
Sammy is dreaming of hazel and catkins
And horses and dancing sheep.

A little while later, Sammy wakes up
He wakes up with such a start.
His old horse has arrived and is licking his face
And behind his horse is the cart.

Then Sammy stands up, brushing leaves off his coat
His face is full of surprise.
As he looks at the horse and the horse looks at him
With a mischievous look in his eyes.

Now Sammy gets busy a-loading the hazel
His cart he loads full to the brim.
The horse pulls hard on the old wooden shafts
Down the track as the light gets dim.

The hurdle-maker awaits the load
Fine fences to craft with the sticks.
And Sammy will get in return for his cargo
Three shillings two ones and a six.

Chapter 3

Keepers of the Treasure

One fair morning in early March, Sammy was on his way to Granny Bambridge's to help her till her vegetable garden. Granny came out the door to greet him. There she stood by her cottage door with the sun shining on her white hair and her shawl blowing in the spring breeze. "Hello my dear Sammy," Granny said. In her hands she held a piping hot loaf of bread fresh from the oven. "Mmmm," Sammy stooped to smell the delicious crust. He couldn't help imagining how it might taste with fried eggs and mushrooms. "I know what you're thinking," smiled Granny, "you're just like your Grandfather. That was his favourite breakfast too!" The mention of his Grandfather reminded Sammy of something he had wanted to ask Granny Bambridge for some time. "Granny, are there still wood-gnomes living in Bramley Wood?" Now you might think that that was a strange question for Sammy to ask, but you see Grandfather Bambridge had often told him stories of wood-gnomes he had met when he was a young forester. At home in Sammy's cottage was a painting that hung over the fireplace, which his Grandfather had painted long, long ago. It was of a family of wood-gnomes standing by the biggest fattest old yew tree you could ever imagine. Sammy had spent many an evening resting in his chair staring into that painting. He often wondered if maybe, just maybe, the painting was of gnomes that Grandfather had seen actually seen.

"Come into the kitchen," Granny Bambridge exclaimed, and before you could say fairy foxglove, yellow butter was melting into two slices of hot bread that Granny had just cut. "Now let me tell you this," she said in a whisper while Sammy was munching away. "When Grandfather first saw the wood-gnomes, he didn't even tell me about 'em, for it was to be kept a secret. But he did tell me when he made that painting which you have. I was amazed, even though I never saw 'em for myself. Now whether they are still there or not, I don't know, but I do remember him saying that they lived in the West Wood. Why don't you go and see for yourself, Sammy?" "Granny, you can be sure, the very next time I go to the West Wood, I'll be looking out for that great yew which is in Grandfather's painting!"

A week later, early on a Monday morning, Sammy set off for the wood as usual, gently tapping Alder's sides with his heels. He sang his morning song as they crossed the marsh together.

Clip clop clip clop to the wood
Across the marsh we go.
Alder you're the finest horse
That ever I did know.

Your warmest coat of cream and brown
Your tail swishes to and fro.
Your mane blows sideways in the breeze
When to the wood we go.

Clip clop clip clop through the wood
We'll ride in sun or rain.
And when our work has all been done
Then home we'll ride again.

Inside the little wooden lodge, the foresters sat around the table for their early morning meeting. Jim, the head forester, asked Sammy to go to the Middle Wood to mark some trees for cutting, for the Landlord's barn needed wood a new roof. A shower of rain had left the trees glistening with drips in the cool March air. Sammy and Alder got to the big grassy clearing in the Middle Wood just in time to see several deer disappear into the trees.

Sammy worked fast that morning, for he found the right trees in good time. He marked each one with a band of twine around the trunk and, as he tied the last knot, a dark March cloud dropped a heavy shower upon them like silver beads in a ray of sun. They waited a while in the shelter of an overhanging holly tree. Then, before their very eyes, there appeared the most beautiful rainbow. It looked like a heavenly halo; a bridge of marvellous glowing colour in the dark grey sky over the trees. Sammy thought he could see one end of the rainbow coming down just over the wood to the west. Then he remembered something very special. Something that Granny Bambridge had told him whilst they were sitting on the bench under her apple tree one day. She had told him that if you could find the end of a rainbow, a treasure would be there to behold. Well, it was the end of this rainbow that Sammy could see, and before you could say "Jack by the hedge," Sammy and Alder were off. Their eyes were alive as they galloped into the woods. Over ditches and fallen trees they sprang. Through streams and marshes they waded, but it seemed that as fast as they could run, the rainbow was always just as far away. Just then though, Sammy spotted the end of the rainbow coming straight down between two trees in the distance. "Go Alder, go, go, go!" He shouted. Alder galloped faster than he'd ever galloped before. The wind whistled through Alder's mane and Sammy's beard. Then all of a sudden, Alder's hoof hit a fallen branch. He tripped and tumbled to the ground. Sammy went flying through the air with no horse under him! He somersaulted then there was a 'bump!' as he hit the ground. Rolling over three times, Sammy came to a stop in the middle of a great big prickly gorse bush! All went quiet... "Auch!" Sammy opened his eyes and, looking up, saw Alder's big wet nose poking in through the top of the bush. "Thank you Alder, I'm alright, apart from a few thorns in my hands and knees. What about you?"

Thank goodness they were both alright. Then, as Sammy crawled out from under the bush, something caught his eye. "Well I never..." he whispered in disbelief. Right there in front of him were two little people running away into the hazel wood. They were carrying what looked like a treasure chest between them. The rainbow had now faded away. Sammy stood up quickly and told Alder to stay where he was. Then he ran, following the little people into the hazel wood, as fast has his legs could carry him. He just saw their backs disappearing towards the biggest, fattest old yew tree he'd ever seen, much like the one in the painting! By the time Sammy got there, they had both vanished rather like the rainbow. Sammy sat down on one of the low-hanging branches

of the yew to catch his breath. He looked all around. "Where did they go? Was I just dreaming or did I see what looked like two wood-gnomes running away with a treasure chest between them?" Sammy called out in a kindly voice: "little gnome people, little gnome people. I'm not here to harm you. My name is Sammy. I'm a forester." He sat listening for a while. "Perhaps I'm too close," he thought, so he carefully got off the branch and laid down on the soft ground.

The wind swirled around the top of the old yew tree, tossing the branches to and fro. Then Sammy heard a little creaking noise coming from somewhere in the trunk. He looked up from where he was lying and there, between two roots, he saw a little wooden door that was being pushed open slowly. Four little fingers were clutching the edge. Then came one of the most wonderful moments of Sammy's whole life! There, standing in the doorway, was a real wood-gnome! Sammy blinked three times and smiled a big smile. Now he knew for sure that Gandfather Bambridge was right. There really are gnomes in Bramley Wood! They looked at each other a while, he and the gnome, and then the gnome took three small steps towards Sammy and spoke: "Did you say Sammy?" He asked in the strangest accent. "Yes, that's right, I'm Sammy."

"And who was your grandfather?" The gnome asked. "Grandfather Bambridge," Sammy replied. As soon as he heard that, the gnome was so excited that he took off his red pointed hat, whirled it around in the air doing a little dance as he did so. He turned around, still dancing, and called out something through the door. Then, in no time at all, many little faces peered over roots and through holes in the tree. The gnomes were shy, as very rarely did they ever get so close to a human being. One by one though, they all came out and stood staring silently at Sammy.

Wood-gnomes are really quite small, only the size of a foot and their babies barely the size of a toe. Now can you imagine how big Sammy would have looked to such tiny people?

A very old gnome then appeared at the door with a walking stick in each hand. All the others turned their eyes to him as he began to speak. In a quivering voice he explained to all: "Grandfather Bambridge often came here to visit us, for he was our friend and hero. As you all know, 'tis only us gnomes who can find the end of a rainbow and so it is our work to collect and guard the treasure which is to be found there. But then one day long ago the bad witch followed us back to the yew tree. She tried to steal the treasure from us but we managed to get it back to our hiding place just in time. She was so angry that she went away to get a big saw to cut down the yew, our beloved home. But Grandfather Bambridge happened to see her steal the saw from the foresters lodge. He followed her all the way here to the old yew and saw her trying to cut it down. "Look," said the elderly gnome, pointing to the bottom of the tree. "The saw mark is still there. Grandfather Bambridge was a very brave and good man. He managed to catch the bad witch by her hands and feet, and out of the forest he took her, back to her cave on the dark wild moor, far beyond the North Wood. She has never returned to this tree since but it is said that she is seen in the wood around the dark October nights. So, everyone, three cheers for Gandfather Bambridge. Hip hip hurrah, hip hip hurrah, hip hip hurrahhh!! And welcome to his Grandson, Sammy the Forester!" They all clapped.

The old wood-gnome hobbled slowly over to Sammy and, putting his hand into a brown cloth-sack that was tied to his waist, he brought out a small stone that glistened green and gold in the palm of his hand. "This is a rainbow treasure, a gift for you, our friend," said the old gnome with a smile. It will guard you in times of danger. Just hold the stone in your hand and think of all the colours of the rainbow." Just then, they heard a big neigh and stamping hooves echo through the woods. "That's Alder, my horse, he wants to go home. It is time to bid you farewell," said Sammy as he stood up, thanking them heartily for his gift. "Please come again!" They all shouted. "I have just one request for you Sammy," said the old gnome, "tell nobody of our meeting. Let it be a secret." "Oh yes, I promise and I will come again," Sammy said as he waved them goodbye.

Sammy patted dear Alder when he found him waiting where he'd left him. "You are a good horse!" He said to him lovingly. Sammy was filled with wonder as he rode back to his homely cottage, past the lapwings and the swaying cotton grasses on the quiet moor. He held the green and gold stone gently in the palm of his strong hand.

* * *

Sun Shines Warm upon the Ground

Sun shines warm upon the ground
Still damp with the early rain.
The people of Bramley are tilling the land
For it's time to start planting again.

They pull up the weeds, they dig in the compost
They talk and they sing as they go.
They rake the ground smooth and then with their fingers
They plant the seed row after row.

Then after the sun and a little more rain
And quite a few days have gone past.
The villagers patiently watch the ground
Until little new shoots come at last.

They kneel on the earth to take a good look
New leaves are about to unfold.
They touch them tenderly with their fingers
And hope the night won't be too cold.

John looked at Jim and Jim looked at Isabel
Isabel looked at Louise.
They all felt a shiver and put on their gloves
And agreed that tonight it could freeze.

Well what do you think they said to each other
Should we cover the plants up with straw?
They all thought about it and nodded their heads
So they went to get plenty and more.

Straw for the carrots, straw for the beans
Straw for to keep off the frost.
Cover them up to keep them from freezing
In case they should all be lost.

The frost it did come and the plants were all saved
Thank goodness they covered 'em then.
The last thing they wanted was more hard work
Of having to plant them again.

Chapter 4

Old Roland

Old Roland lived in a small thatched cottage on the edge of the River Mistle, deep in Bramley Wood. Roland was very old, just a few weeks short of 101. He had lived in the wood all his life and accepted little help from anyone apart from his dear wife, who had long since passed away.

One morning in the spring, Roland wandered down to the riverbank, as he often did. The night sky had been starry and still. Now the dawn glistened with pink and silvery blue in the rising sun. Roland could hear many birds of the water calling from the reed beds up the river. So, very slowly and carefully, he got into his wooden boat and rowed under the overhanging willows, hoping to see the first newly hatched chicks. He stopped his boat in a deep lily pool near the reed bed, and sure enough there was a speckled mallard duck swimming along with her five little chicks. This made Roland very happy! Then, with a smile on his face and the warm spring sun on his chest, he lay back in his boat and soon, as old people sometimes do, he fell fast asleep.

Now, slowly but surely, his boat began to drift from the pool and back into the river's moving current. Then, before long, Roland had unknowingly drifted past his cottage, around the bend in the river and into the next pool, where a fox stood lapping up some water with its pink tongue. It looked up for a while and sniffed the air as Roland floated past. At that moment, a green woodpecker flew right overhead with its loud laughing-like call ringing out over the water. You would have thought Old Roland would have heard that... But he didn't and now his boat was fast drifting towards the entrance of the river cave!

Well, it just so happened that Sammy the Forester was riding his cream and brown dappled horse along the edge of the hazel wood, high above the river cave. He looked down below and just caught sight of Old Roland before he disappeared into the darkness of the cave. Sammy called as loud as he could: "Roland! Roland! Roland!" And do you think he woke up?

The boat drifted into the cool dark cave. Drips ran down the walls and fell from the ceiling to the water. Plip...plip...plop...plip. All else was silent. Soon however, not so far ahead, there was a strange flickering light dancing on the ceiling of the cave and the sound of someone humming a tune. A wood-gnome had come down a long stone staircase with his oil-lamp, to fetch water in a leather bucket. He soon stopped humming when he saw an old wooden boat drifting past in the dark water of the river. Gnomes are too short to see over the sides of boats so he called out: "Anybody there? Anybody there?" Old Roland, still fast asleep, just turned over to make himself more comfortable.

Somewhere high overhead, in the hazel wood, Sammy was riding in haste through bog and bramble, ditch and bank, towards the other end of the river cave. Could he get there in time?

Quite soon, the boat drifted towards a small dot of light that got bigger and bigger, brighter and brighter. Then, all of a sudden, the boat was flooded with sunlight and warm air as it reappeared into the beauty of the spring morning. A slender brown trout with its speckled back and quivering fins hovered still in the fast-moving current under the boat. Above Roland was the high stone bridge over which the seven foresters would pass on their way to and from the wood. Sitting on a mossy stone, fishing beside a deep swirling pool, was a man dressed in a long green jacket, a felt hat and tall boots. Next to him was an open canvas fishing bag. It was Lord Hart Williams of Bramley Manor! It just so happened that, at that moment, as Roland drifted by, the landlord looked down through his enormous grey moustache, to tread a worm onto his hook. Roland bobbed along out of sight. "Ahh, that's got it!" The Landlord said to himself, and cast his line back into the water. The Landlord could then hear the sound of hooves on gravel. Sammy appeared suddenly on the bridge. He called to the Landlord with an urgent voice: "Have you seen Old Roland come past in his boat, Sir?" "Oh no," said the Landlord, "and anyway he would never come as far as this." Sammy explained to the Landlord what he had seen. He looked up and thought for a moment. "Good day Sir," said Sammy to the Landlord as he started on his way deep into the hazel wood, to where the wood-gnomes live.

Old Roland's boat bumped against a tree root as it entered the next pool in the river. But even that didn't wake him up! He had a big smile on his face as he dreamt of the little ducklings, which he had seen earlier that morning. A black and white cat that lived in the nearby Bramley Station was crouched down low on a fallen tree next to the river. It had been watching a brown water vole on the far bank, which disappeared quickly as the boat came past.

Then, around the next corner, everything changed. Roland's boat looked smaller as it drifted towards the middle of the much bigger River Toe. Bramley Wood was now behind him and Roland was passing Mistletoe Mill. The big waterwheel was not turning, for at that moment Richard the Miller was somewhere below the first floor, greasing all the cogwheels and bearings. His wife Flo was in the kitchen making bread, which was to go into the hot redbrick oven next to the fireplace. Do you think the Miller or his wife saw Old Roland? No, and would you believe it Old Roland was now drifting slowly towards the sea!

The weather was fair and the air was filled with the sound of lapwings and curlews. Then, quite soon, the boat drifted close to a long bed of bulrushes and there, standing on its long thin legs in the rippled water, was a tall grey heron. It had been waiting patiently in the gentle breeze for a passing fish. Then there was a long loud whistle in the distance. Soon there was the sound of hissing and chuffing and the clackety clack of wheels on rails as the scolding hot black engine pulling six dark red coaches came thundering by with a thick plume of grey-white smoke like a storm cloud overhead. It was the 9:45 train on its way from Bramley to Cyderton-on-Sea. At that moment, the fireman was busy shovelling jagged chunks of dusty black coal into the white-hot firebox. His blue shirt was soaked with sweat. The engine driver was tapping the pressure gauge with a spanner. Neither of them saw Old Roland in his boat on the river down below. However, standing on a seat next to a partly opened window in one the coaches was a girl in a red dress. Her eyes were half shut and her hair blowing in every direction. She saw the big grey heron flying across the river and a wooden boat with an old man fast asleep in it. She turned and said to her mother: "Look, look Ma, on the river!" "Just a moment, dear," her mother said, as she was finishing reading a line in her book. It was too late! She'd missed it!

Roland had just dreamt that his kettle was boiling and going along on wheels! He chuckled in his sleep.

As Roland drifted around the next bend, the river got wider and wider. On Roland's left there were endless miles of marshland. Straight ahead, there was the calm open sea, and to his right was the entrance of Cyderton Harbour, with the harbourmaster's cottage nearby at the end of the harbour wall. The harbourmaster was patching some holes in his sails at that moment, when there was a loud blast from the train's whistle as it approached Cyderton Station. He jumped up on his upturned boat to see the train, and looked at his watch. "Three minutes late!" He said to himself.

You'd have thought the harbourmaster would have seen Old Roland! Perhaps he may have, had the train been on time, but now Old Roland drifted around the other side of the harbour wall and out into the open sea! Now all that could be heard were seagulls crying in the harbour, a dog barking far away and little waves breaking all around the boat.

Could it now be that poor Old Roland would be lost at sea forever? Was there really no-one else out there who may see him and save his life? Well, actually there was... There was hope for Old Roland in the shape of a high round stone tower that was painted white and was built on rocks that stuck out of the water like the teeth of a shark. It was the Cyderton

Lighthouse. Yes, there it stood like a tall white vase on the water with its high shimmering windows in the sunlit sky. There came Old Roland floating by in his wooden boat in the salty sea air.

The lighthouse keeper had been polishing the lenses behind the lamps all morning whilst keeping half an eye on the sea. He was about to take a break and go out onto the balcony, when his nose caught the smell of something burning. "Oh no! My porridge!" He shouted. He threw down his rags and ran as fast as he could down the spiral staircase to the kitchen where he grabbed the handle of his blackened saucepan and crackling porridge. By the time he had scrubbed the saucepan clean and made more porridge, Old Roland had drifted far out of sight.

Even if he awoke right now, what could he do? Clouds were gathering on the horizon and the breeze was getting stronger.

Then, deep in the dark green water beneath Roland's boat, a black shape was moving quickly. Very soon a feathery head and neck appeared with a silver and blue fish flipping in its long yellow beak. It paddled its way towards the boat and flew up onto the bow, swallowed the fish whole then peered down at Roland with deep shiny eyes. The surprise visitor was a cormorant, a wonderful master of the air and the water, which had decided to use Roland's boat as a resting place to eat its fish and dry its feathers. It stretched its wings out wide into the sea breeze, droplets of salty water falling onto the weathered wood. Then, slowly the boat began to turn and head in a different direction. It was now moving towards the land! The cormorant's wings had become a sail! Gradually the land got nearer and nearer until the bottom of the boat was put down gently on the sand by a small wave. The cormorant flew back out to sea. Just then, two big strong hands pulled the boat from the water and onto the beach. It was Sammy the Forester of course!

Sammy somehow knew all along that Roland must have passed the Landlord by the bridge, but then he knew for sure when he heard that a wood-gnome had seen the boat in the river cave. At that moment, Sammy followed the river towards the sea.

It just so happened that some fishermen had come to mend their nets on the beach. The fishermen gave Sammy a hand to gently lift the boat, with Roland still fast asleep in it, onto Sammy's cart.

Sammy rode carefully back to Bramley Wood. When he arrived at Roland's cottage, he reversed the cart into the river. Then, when the boat was afloat, he tied it up to a willow branch in its usual place by the riverbank. Sammy went into Roland's cottage, stoked up the fire with fresh wood and put the kettle on. He took two cups of tea back down to the boat. He could see that Roland had just woken up and was chuckling to himself. "Hello Roland," said Sammy. "I must have fallen asleep," said Roland "and I have had the funniest dream! I dreamt my kettle was boiling and going along on wheels."

"Fancy that!" Said Sammy with a big smile, handing Roland his cup of tea. Together they sat in the boat and talked of things of the forest for good while. Then Sammy went back to his work in the woods.

Chapter 5

The Honeydew Ponds

It was the month of March and for many weeks great puffy clouds had been gathered together over the moor, as if all the world were wrapped in cotton wool. Every day the sun had been rising a little higher above those clouds until one morning, soon after church as the clock struck 11, golden rays of sunlight pushed all the clouds away and the land lit up as brightly as the song of the thrush.

Isabel could feel the warm sun on her shoulders as she carried a pail of fresh water and a bunch of parsley into the cottage. She went back out with a basket of washing, followed by Gabriel with a bag of pegs. "Come on let's get the washing hung, then we'll go for a walk," said Isabel. Gabriel passed his mum the pegs, one by one. Then soon they made their way towards the marsh track. When they got to the village pond, they stood for a while, watching the busy ducks making their nests in the reeds. Then came a friendly "hello" from Old John Drew who lived in the last cottage by the pond. "This weather is set to last a week," he said with delight in his soft voice.

The children of the village called him Weather John. That was because he always seemed to know what sort of weather was coming. One day,

when a group of children were gathered around him near Christmas time, he told them that it would soon snow. "How do you know that?" Asked Samantha, who was the teacher's daughter. "Ah well," he said, "I can just feel it in my bones." The children always wondered how he could do that. "Some people just can," explained Samantha's mum.

Gabriel looked up at Weather John's old wrinkled face and his big bushy white sideburns. His deep brown eyes were looking at the boy with a twinkle from under the brim of his black hat. Then he asked with a smile, "Are you on your way to the woods?" Gabriel nodded a yes. "Now, if you go to the honeydew ponds in the South Wood, you might see the water fairies. Ahh, but only children can see 'em mind you!" Gabriel's face lit up! "Well off you go then, I'll keep my fingers crossed," said Old Weather John, one finger over the other.

Mother and son both set off over the marsh track, skipping around all the muddy puddles. One puddle was so big that Isabel put Gabriel on her back, gathered her skirt and ran through the water quickly before it seeped into her leather boots. Sometimes they ran up to the puddles and jumped right over them. They were having great fun! By the time they got to Bramley Wood, they were quite puffed out. They walked up the hill and onto the South Wood track they went. There were the green shoots of bluebells on both sides.

Isabel looked at some primrose flowers. She took in a deep breath. Gabriel did the same. Ahh, spring is nearly here! A bumblebee buzzed around the primroses, collecting pollen to take back to her new home in a hollow tree root nearby.

Soon they found the Honeydew Ponds at the edge of the downy birch wood. There were two ponds surrounded by myrtle plants, heather and gorse bushes. Near the edge of the water were some big grey weathered stones covered with lichen and moss. "Dad told me that adders live here," said Gabriel. So, just in case, they jumped on the ground and clapped their hands, but they both got a fright as a grey heron leaped into the air close by and flew over the trees. The two of them sat on a stone, warmed by the sun and shared some bread and cheese. "I'm so glad we came," Isabel said. She sat and knitted happily on this fine March day while Gabriel wandered through the heather to the edge of the pond.

He stood watching the water twinkle in the sunlight....and look! Four swans were on the other side. Two of them were pecking in the water and the other two were doing the same in the ripples, only upside down. Gabriel smiled to himself as he realised that they were their reflections. Then he looked down by his feet on the bank next to the pond. He saw fluffy white clouds mirrored in the water, but then he saw something else. He laid down on his tummy to take a closer look and there before his eyes was quite a different world. The water was crystal clear and he could see the most wonderful underwater garden. There were rocks and sticks and fallen leaves hovering in the green light. Strange plants hung still in the water making long shadows on the bottom. Just then, something came swimming along with its legs kicking, making the birch leaves dance and twirl around the rocks. It was a slim green frog passing through. Then Gabriel noticed some tiny bubbles coming out from a little cave by a root. A newt came along and rested on the root. Time stood still a while as Gabriel stared dreamily into the newt's eye. The tiny bubbles stopped and then started again. Then came a most wondrous sight! A little hand with long fingers appeared from the cave. Its fingers began to stroke one of the newt's feet. Then came a head with beautiful golden hair that swirled around slowly in the water. Soon her arms and whole body appeared. There she sat on a stone by the cave with long wings folded down her back. Her silver dress was laced with gold and green. Gabriel looked on with open mouth. "A water fairy! I can see a water fairy!" He held his breath as wonder filled his body. Gabriel noticed that she had long feet with webbed toes, like those of a frog or newt, and had now found herself a comfortable place on her lap. Tiny bubbles were coming from her nose, for it was so that these little beings could breathe under water. The local folk have always said that these beings lived in fairy caves somewhere underneath the downy birch trees, and that they swam through underwater tunnels from one pond to another.

Gabriel lay on the heather by the pond's edge watching the beautiful fairy. Isabel was laying on the warm rock watching her beautiful son when Gabriel turned his head and beckoned to her with a whisper, "Mum, Mum come over here quick, I can see a water fairy!" She hurried over and lay next to him. "Look down there!" She looked carefully but could only see a newt swimming away. "A fairy was there," Gabriel said, "I know she was there, I saw her!" He tried to peer into the cave then glanced across the water for a moment wondering where she might have gone. He saw only the four swans and the downy birch trees at the edge of the sunlit pond.

"I do believe you saw them," said Isabel as they walked back to the forest gate. "Do you remember what Weather John told us? He said only children can see the water fairies." "Do you think Weather John has seen them?" Asked Gabriel. "Well, you could ask him," said his mum.

It was already dusk when they got back to Bramley Village. The sun was setting behind the woods in the distance. Old Weather John was just shutting his chickens in as Gabriel ran up to him. With a smile he asked the boy eagerly, "Seen any water fairies then?" "Yes, yes!" Said Gabriel excitedly, telling Weather John everything that had happened. "Have you ever seen the water fairies, Weather John?" The old man looked up at the rising moon and closed his eyes a while. "Now if I remember rightly," said he, "the one I saw had webbed feet like those of a frog or perhaps a newt... Ahh, and golden hair that swirled around in the water.... yes and wings that trailed down the back....oh and a silver frock with green and gold..." He paused for a while then looked down into Gabriel's shiny eyes. "When I became a young man I could see 'em no more. I felt very sad for a while but I've always treasured this memory and am so happy that children can still see 'em." What a wonderful end to the day! They thanked Weather John and went home. Gabriel couldn't wait to tell Sammy!

Long after Gabriel had fallen asleep that night and the full moon had risen over Bramley Wood lighting up the white feathers of the swans and the bark of the downy birch trees, seven little heads appeared around a water lily in the pond and, like damsel flies, they rose up above the surface. Droplets of water falling from their beating wings, they stepped upon the lily leaf with joined hands. Then the circle of water fairies gently flew among the swans and the downy birch. And there, in the moonlight, they played and danced with such joy until the very first signs of dawn. Then, one by one, they slipped back into the water quietly, so as not to awaken the sleeping newts and frogs.

Chapter 6

Rose's Missing Ring

For many of the women in Bramley village, washing day was on a Monday. There was a group of stone cottages by the village green that all had their own little flower gardens. The families shared a big cobbled yard that had a row of washhouses, drying lines and a well.

One fine Monday morning in May the women were walking to and fro with buckets of water from the well to fill the copper boilers in the washhouses. Nine buckets each one took. Then fires were lit underneath to heat the water. Smoke billowed from each chimney as the dirty cotton sheets were pushed into the scolding water with long wooden tongs. A mother song thrush was perched on a heavy iron mangle before flying to her nest in the nearby holly tree with a beak full of worms for her babies.

Among the busy women was Samantha's Auntie Rose. She appeared from the last cottage in the row. Wearing her brown dress, she carried a large basket overflowing with washing in both hands. Her baby son was safely on her back, looking over her shoulder at all the excitement in the sunlit yard. Rose wore a beautiful golden ring on her finger that had once belonged to her great grandmother. It had a fine ruby set in the centre and would glow deep red on such a sunny day. There was a stone on top of the gate pillar in the yard that was shaped like a bowl. In this stone bowl Rose always placed her ring on washing day, often admiring its beauty as she walked by.

"Tea up!" Shouted one of the women through an open window. Then they all disappeared inside. Now there was only the sound of crackling fires and chatter in the kitchen.

It wasn't so long before a visitor from the air suddenly dropped into the yard. Great black wings a-spread and hooked claws, it landed on the edge of the well, peering into the still water far below with deep black eyes looking down its sharp grey beak. All the other birds disappeared except for one brave robin redbreast, which stayed put in the brilliant white blossom of a pear tree nearby. The big black feathered bird turned its head in sudden movements, looking the yard up and down. Then something caught its eye. It lowered its body, stretched its wings then with a jump it flew across to the stone pillar by the gate. In a flash, up and over the cottage roofs the great bird did fly with something red glistening in its beak, leaving only a draft in the air and a tail feather on the cobblestones.

The women soon returned to the yard chatting happily. They ran piles of wet washing through the mangles and soon the sparkling white sheets filled the yard, swaying gently in the warm May breeze. Then there was a cry of despair. It was Rose. "My ring, my ring," she screamed, "it's gone!" All the women stopped what they were doing and looked over to Rose, for they all knew how Rose so loved that ring. From that moment, the washing was stopped and every square inch of the cobbled yard was searched. Where on earth could it be? They searched high and

low, crawling up and down on the cobbles until their knees turned red. Poor Rose was so desperate to find her precious ring that she looked everywhere all at once. She kept seeing it in the stone bowl on the pillar even though it wasn't there. She squeezed her finger hard to comfort it from the loss as tears rolled down her cheeks.

The oldest lady amongst them, Alice Greenhill, who was 86 years-old, sat on a wooden chair by the door. She began to think carefully and slowly about the missing ring. Now this wasn't the first time she'd seen this kind of thing in her long life and there was nearly always a simple answer awaiting among the panic and despair. Old Alice stayed on that chair by the door, long after the others had given up and gone in to comfort Rose with a cup of tea. She watched the last rays of the setting sun run down the cottage walls like golden honey, and then she saw a big black raven fly low over the rooftops in the twilight sky. It was returning to its nest in the top of the great elm tree on the green to roost for the night. Alice looked at the bowl-shaped stone on the pillar. Then she noticed that near her feet was the jet-black tail feather of a raven. "Hmm, I wonder..." she thought. "Could it be, could it just be....that this raven has taken Rose's ring back to its nest in the top of the great elm tree?" She gazed up at the tree and thought for a moment. "Well, there's only one way we're ever going to find out." Alice Greenhill stood up, feeling a little hope for Rose.

She was about to go in when she heard footsteps down the narrow alleyway. She turned and there was Gabriel walking past the yard. "Hello Auntie Greenhill," he said with a smile. "Hello dear," said Alice, "has your father returned home from work yet?" "Oh yes," said Gabriel, "we've just finished supper." "Would you ask him if he would be so kind as to come over to see me?" "Of course," said Gabriel, "I'll ask him right away." Soon after, Sammy's smiling face appeared at Alice's window. "What can I do for you Alice?" Sammy asked. Alice invited him in and told him all about the missing ring and her thoughts about the raven. "Do you think you would be able and willing to climb up to that raven's nest at the top of the elm tree?" She asked. "Like you used to when you were a lad?" "Well, I'm willing to give it a go, but it is a long way up," said Sammy. "I wouldn't like to fall because it is just as long a way down." Sammy agreed to do the climb on Saturday morning, first thing. "Perhaps we shouldn't mention it to Rose. We don't want to get her hopes up too high yet," said Alice, wisely.

Saturday came around and Sammy was first up. He stood in his front garden gazing up at the giant elm tree. The more he looked at it, the higher it seemed. Just then, the raven took off from its nest and flew towards the meadow behind the manor house. After breakfast, Sammy and Gabriel went to the foot of the great elm on the green. Its trunk was so wide that you could stand fifteen people shoulder to shoulder in a circle around it. Sammy had brought his ladder so as to reach the first branches. Then, as they started to climb, Sammy leading the way, along came John the Blacksmith and Jim the Head Forester, with Alice, Samantha and Isabel. "Take your time and be careful!" Shouted Jim. It wasn't long before the word got around and most of the villagers of Bramley gathered at the bottom of the tree to watch.

Soon, Sammy and Gabriel had climbed high enough to see right over their cottage and into the meadow at the back where Alder stood swishing his tail. Sammy and Gabriel looked down at the people far below and waved. They then looked up at the nest, which still appeared to be just as high as it was from the ground. Their muscles were stiffened as they heaved themselves higher into the arms of the great elm. They had now climbed so high that they were well above the manor house and even the church tower. The branches of the tree were getting thinner and the raven's nest nearer. They both rested a while, looking up at the big twiggy nest overhead. Then they peered around at the wonderful view of the village. They could see right down into all the gardens of every cottage in Bramley. The only building that was higher than them was the windmill on the grassy Rye Tor to the south. "Look," said Sammy, pointing to the north-west. To their surprise, they could see the church spire at Ciderton-on-Sea in the distance. Sammy then pointed to the east, at a huge grey and white cloud towering high in the sky. "I hope that's not coming our way," he said to Gabriel, looking a little anxious. Sammy climbed a few feet higher and stopped. He looked down at Gabriel. "That's as far as I can go son," he said. "The next branches will be too thin to take my weight." "It's up to you now Gabriel. Do you think you can do it?" "Yes Dad, I can!" The big woody nest swayed to and fro in the breeze as Gabriel climbed the last bit. He put one foot in a forked branch under the nest and held onto another above it. Gabriel pulled himself up high enough to peer into the nest, where he could see four beautiful eggs in the heather lined cradle of the raven. "Watch out!" Shouted Sammy. Gabriel looked up, and right before his eyes were two great wings and a mass of black feathers in the shape of a furious raven! It pecked his jacket and circled around angrily. "Hold on tight!" Shouted Sammy. Gabriel quickly ran his fingers all around the nest while the angry raven kept swooping and squawking around him. "Better come down!" Sammy called out. "The raven needs to keep its eggs warm and you might get pecked." Gabriel had one last search and then came back down to join his father.

The raven soon returned to her eggs. By now, Gabriel's arms were getting very tired. Just then, they heard a voice shouting out from down below them. It was Jim, the Head Forester: "How are you doing up there?" "Gabriel's arms are getting tired now," Sammy replied. Well, it wasn't long before Jim came climbing up the tree with a long length of rope over his shoulder. He fastened it around Gabriel with a special knot, put the rest over a strong branch and let it fall to the ground. "Hey John, are you ready to take the rope? Gabriel needs a hand down," shouted Jim. "Got it secured!" John the Blacksmith shouted back. "Alright, it's safe for you to let go now Gabriel," said Jim. Gabriel let himself drop and hung like a spider on a web whilst John the Blacksmith slid the rope gently through his strong hands until Gabriel landed softly on the ground. Sammy and Jim's feet soon appeared on the ladder. All the villagers gave a cheer of relief, now that they were safely down. Father and son got a big hug from Isabel.

As Jim began to coil up the rope, there was Rose standing before them with a look of hope in her eyes. And then she just had to ask: "What was it like in the nest? Where there many eggs? Did you find anything else up there?" They'd been so busy getting down the tree that Sammy had forgotten all about the ring. He turned to look at Gabriel who had a big smile from ear to ear. And there between his fingers was Rose's beautiful ruby ring. Rose was so happy to see it that she held it to her heart with one hand and gave Gabriel a great big hug with the other. The whole crowd of villagers gave a big round of applause as tears of joy fell from Rose's eyes. At that moment came a big gust of wind and the rain poured heavy upon the ground. "That was a bit of luck," shouted Sammy as the villagers dashed for shelter. High up in the great elm, the raven spread her warm body gently over her four precious eggs.

From that day on, Rose always put the ring on a chain around her neck on washing days. She could never thank Sammy and Gabriel enough for their brave deed and she had learnt from old Alice that there was very often a simple answer to life's many questions.

The raven raised four fine chicks in her nest that year and, of course, she would never have known how much that ring meant to Rose.

Chapter 7

The Singing Poppies

It was three days before midsummer. Poppies grew rich red all around Patrick O'Donovan's caravan. They swayed gently in the breeze as the hot sun shone through their delicate petals.

When the evening came and all was still, Patrick hung his kettle over the fire as the big orange sun set over the beech wood. He could feel the cool air of the evening on his skin and smell the camomile flowers that grew on the side of the forest track. This reminded him of his childhood home many, many years ago in the West of Ireland, far away across the sea. Sadly, as the years had passed, Patrick became blind, but being a man of the land who loved to use his hands, he learned to turn pieces of forest wood into chairs and tables.

Now, although he was blind, he could hear everything. He could hear the little birds' breath as they ran up and down the tree trunks collecting spiders. He could hear the tiny feet of mice running under him through their tunnels. He could even hear ants brushing off leafmould from their feet beneath his caravan. Patrick indeed felt happy in his old wooden home by the side of the track to the West Wood, being among all the natural things in the forest.

The old Irishman poured himself a mug of tea and stretched back in his wooden chair near the fire. Just then, Patrick thought he could hear something. It was the sweetest sound of singing voices coming from nearby. He got off his chair and slowly went down on his hands and knees. Tilting his head, he listened very carefully. Now remember, Patrick could hear everything! He crawled gingerly among the poppies, catching their fragrance as he went by, all the while listening out for the voices. Just then, he realized the sweet sound was coming from inside the poppy flowers! Patrick was filled with joy! He felt as if he was floating weightlessly with such beautiful song.

Then came the sound of hooves and wheels on the gravel track. Sammy and Alder were on their way back to the forest lodge after a long day's work. Patrick rose up on his knees. "Sammy, Sammy! Come here and listen to this." Sammy hopped down off his cart and went over to Patrick. "What can you hear?" He asked. "Put your ear to the poppies," said Patrick. Sammy did so but he could hear nothing. He tried over and over again but he still heard nothing. Patrick felt so sad that he couldn't share the beautiful singing with Sammy. With a sigh he bid Sammy goodnight, went into his caravan and closed the door.

When Sammy got home to his cottage in Bramley, he told Isabel of his meeting with Patrick and the singing poppies. "I couldn't hear anything," said Sammy. "I'm sure he could hear the voices," said Isabel. "Although Patrick is blind, he can hear everything you know."

The next day was sunny and warm again and before you could say 'Taxasbecatafestidiata', all the children of Bramley had heard about the singing poppies. Soon they gathered together under the great elm tree

on the village green and excitedly they set off across the marsh hoping to hear the singing poppies of Bramley Wood. As they crossed the brow of the hill, at the top of the western slope of the wood, they saw the roof of Patrick's old wooden caravan, and a wisp of smoke rising from his fire. Patrick was rubbing oil into a chair he had made that morning. He knew the children would arrive soon, as he had heard them already from a long way off. Patrick welcomed the children with a big smile. They had brought him gifts of eggs and potatoes from the village. He was filled with great delight when they asked him about the singing poppies. Patrick put his finger to his lips. "Shhh, come quietly and listen carefully." The children crawled among the poppies and put their ears to the bright red petals for quite a while. Some of them thought they could hear the singing very faintly, others could only hear the skylarks high above. But they could smell the fragrance of the flowers and feel the hot sun on their backs.

All the while a little wood mouse with pointed ears had been sitting at the base of an old elder tree watching the children. Patrick had heard it grooming its fur with its little paws earlier on.

When it was time to go home, Patrick thanked the children once again for their generous gifts as they set off through the woods. They all arrived back in Bramley quiet and filled with a sense of mystery. The children slept deep and long that night. Whilst in the land of their dreams, Sammy and Isabel where out in the barn working, for they were making something. Quite a strange thing it was too, all made of hazel sticks and rhubarb leaves. It stood as tall as Isabel and looked like a giant cow horn. It had a small hole at one end and a great big one at the other. When Sammy whispered into the small hole it was so loud at the other end that it made the woodworms drill even deeper into the rafters. "Well, that should do it!" Said Isabel, laughing, still blocking her ears.

The next day was midsummer, the longest day of the year. A time that all the country-folk would celebrate in the days of Sammy the Forester. Gabriel awoke early that morning. Before he got out of his bed, he watched the many swallows in the blue sky darting and diving for flies. He noticed that there were already a lot of folks standing on the village green. They were looking at a strange giant horn lying on the grass. "What could that be?" He asked himself. Quick as a flash, Gabriel ran to the green, still in his pyjamas. Sammy and Isabel were not telling anybody what the giant horn was for, but they were inviting all the villagers to follow them up to the wood to celebrate midsummer with Patrick O'Donovan.

As the evening drew near, the good folk of Bramley put on their finest clothes. The cheery villagers followed Sammy, who carried the giant horn on his shoulders across the sunlit marsh to the green wood above.

Patrick was excited, for he had already heard them laughing and chattering on the marsh two miles away. When, finally, the procession arrived, Patrick was standing next to the glow of his fire, wearing his finest hat and greeting them with a happy tune on his fiddle. The villagers all gathered round the fire and prepared potatoes and trout to roast in the embers. A visitor then took the whole village by surprise. For Jim the Head Forester had brought Old Roland with him, who was comfortable in his armchair on the back of Jim's horse and cart. Even Martha appeared. She was sitting with her back towards the elder tree, a basket of flowers resting in her lap.

Sammy drove four hazel poles into the ground and carefully tied the giant horn onto them as everyone watched curiously. Isabel delicately pushed one of the poppy flowers up through the small hole of the horn.

Just then, the little fairy wood mouse with the pointed ears that had watched everything, ran past Martha's shoe and disappeared down the hole in the roots of the elder tree. Martha smiled as she watched him go. He ran through many tunnels under the ground and appeared from under a hawthorn root in the fairy world. The sky in the fairy world was made of earth and roots strewn with crystals of every colour and shape, which twinkled and shone like the stars. The ground was of misty ponds and soft golden leaves laced with seeds of every kind. Just nearby in the silvery light of many glowworms was a circle of fairies and standing in the middle was the queen of all the fairies holding her wand high. When she saw the fairy mouse, she beckoned him to her. He made a bow then stood on his hind legs, placing his paws in her hands. The other fairies could not hear what he whispered in her ear. "Oh, that's lovely," said the fairy queen with a smile. She whispered something back to the mouse. She then raised her wand and the fairies began singing the most beautiful song. The song filled the air; it went down under the water to the fairy fish, up in the air to the fairy moths and up, up into the roots that hung from the fairy sky. Now some of those roots were the roots of the beech, and some were the roots of the elder, some were of the holly ... and some were the roots of the poppies ... ahhh, the ones that just happened to grow all around Patrick's caravan.

The beautiful enchanting voices travelled up the roots of the poppies. One of these roots went up to the stem, which went up to its beautiful red flower that went up through the hole in the giant horn. At that moment, Patrick raised his arms up into the air: "My wonderful friends," he said. "Listen, listen!" Everyone went quiet. Then softly the sound of the sweetest voices came crystal clear out of the giant horn. The villagers were astonished. The sound became louder and even more beautiful. The people took each other by the hand and began to dance. They danced in circles, they danced in pairs, they danced and danced around the poppies in the light of the fire, under the midsummer night sky. They danced with their hearts filled with joy until they could dance no more. Then, just as the tip of the big golden moon rose over the moor, all went quiet. The singing had stopped. Soon, all that could be heard was an owl somewhere deep in the wood and the breathing of all the colourful people of Bramley as they lay huddled around the smouldering fire fast asleep. The poppies bowed their heads silently over them and the little fairy mouse lay sleeping in his nest somewhere under the roots of the elder tree. Nobody ever did know where that beautiful music came from, except for the little fairy wood mouse of course, and perhaps Martha, and now you know something too. And as for the people of Bramley, well, the midsummer mystery lived on and on.

Chapter 8

Lost in the Wood

One very fine afternoon in July, the Landlady of Bramley Village decided to ride her silky black horse into the wood. Weather John was repairing his gate as she rode past. "Good morning Lady Hart Williams," he called with a smile, raising his hat a little. She returned the greeting and then asked: "Mr Drew, what do you think of this lovely sunshine? Will it last?" "Certainly, for the rest of the week, m'lady," replied Weather John as he looked out all across the bright blue sky.

Lady Hart Williams rode sidesaddle over the dried moor to the sound of skylarks and hooves that kicked up red dust from the baked track. She smiled, enjoying the freedom of the moor and the breeze that blew through her flowing clothes. She rode deep into Bramley Wood, but then she took a wrong turn and lost her way. The track narrowed and turned into scrubland but still she kept riding, hoping she would get to the edge of the wood before long. It was then that Lady Hart Williams saw a giant oak tree growing in a rocky hollow near a stream. Being thirsty she got off her horse and took a long drink. Then, as she lifted her head from the water, she thought she could hear the strangest music coming faintly from the oak tree. The music made her horse nervous. Suddenly it bolted and ran far off into the wood, out of sight. As much as she tried to call him back it was too late, he was gone. "Now how will I get home?" Lady Hart Williams thought to herself.

Despite being without her horse, she was filled with curiosity. She walked carefully towards the tree. "What is this music I'm hearing?" She said in a whisper whilst peering into the rocky hollow. "Well bless my soul…" She said to herself. Lady Hart Williams looked in disbelief, for lying on some soft grass under the oak tree was a small person; a little thin man with pointed ears and big eyes. He was wearing a dark green tunic and his long black hair was tied back with woodbine. He was resting his back on a mossy root and in his lap was a strange musical instrument, which he was playing skilfully. It was made of hollow wood and had four strings. Lady Hart Williams stood tall at the top of the hollow but that didn't seem to bother him. He just looked at her with his big eyes and carried on plucking the four strings. Lady Hart Williams could see that this little person looked just like one of the pixie folk that the villagers had so often spoken of. She had never believed in them, so she was more surprised than ever to meet one! A second pixie then appeared from a little cave in the side of the hollow. This time it was a little thin woman. She held a wooden flute in her hand, wore a brown kilt and had long black hair all down her back. More pixie folk began to appear, all carrying musical instruments the likes of which Lady Hart Williams had never seen.

The sun was beginning to set, casting low shafts of orange light into the hollow. There stood Lady Hart Williams, lost with no horse and feeling chilly in her summer clothes. She was now surrounded by more

than one hundred little pixie folk, whom she had always thought were complete nonsense until that moment! What was to become of poor Lady Hart Williams? She asked them politely if they could please help her find her way out of the wood. But they spoke in a different language to her. Lady Hart Williams sat down on a stone with her feet on the soft grass, gazing at the pixie people in amazement, yet wondering what to do. They walked all about her. Some of them were lighting lamps and others seemed to be forming a circle right around the old oak tree.

Although Lady Hart Williams should by now have tried to find her own way home before nightfall, she began to feel more and more drawn towards the circle of music and light. She couldn't help herself. A family of owls took flight one by one from a hole half way up the oak, disappearing into the darkening wood.

The pixies began to dance. At first, it was all the boys and men folk. They moved slowly around the tree to the strange sound of bows on strings. This went on for quite some time until, all of a sudden, the girls and women folk came busting out from under a big flat stone in the bank. Some had whistles and flutes to their mouths; others had drums in their hands and bells around their ankles. As they joined with the boys and men, they danced together around and around the tree. By now they danced the wildest dance you could ever imagine! What a sound and what a sight! It wasn't long before Lady Hart Williams began to move in time with the music too. Then soon her dance was as wild as that of the pixies. The lanterns flickered as the dancers whirled about the tree.

Now what of Lord Hart Williams? Surely by now the poor man would be very worried about his wife. Indeed, he was! It was night time and

there was no sign of her. And so it was he gathered nine men and nine horses and soon ten little lanterns were seen disappearing over the marsh and into the wood. Sammy led the way up the track towards the forester's lodge. "We must search the wood through and through," said Lord Hart Williams as he pulled up next to Sammy, holding his lantern high.

Meanwhile Lady Hart Williams still danced wildly around the oak tree with the pixies, kicking her legs high in the air as she leapt over a tree root. But suddenly she was taken quite by surprise when someone took her by the hand and pulled her out of the circle. One leg tripped over the other and Lady Hart Williams fell to the ground with a bump. A woman's voice said something sternly to the pixies in their strange language. Then all went quiet… Lady Hart Williams sat up, wiping droplets of sweat from her brow. It was Martha that she saw in the light of the lantern! "Well, well," said Martha with a smile, and "Good evening Lady Hart Williams. Have you enjoyed your dance with the pixies?" "Well yes, but I didn't mean to dance with them. I couldn't help myself. Besides, I'm lost and need to find my way home. My husband will be worried by now." "The pixies are masters at enchanting us big people," said Martha. "And should you join them in dance, well, what you think is a short while could become an hour or even a whole day!"

Sammy and Lord Hart Williams stopped for a while in a clearing. The moon shone brightly on the ground. Then came the sound of hooves galloping towards them on the long grassy path. There was a long loud "neighhh" and before you could say 'ivy leaf toadflax' a silky black horse with saddle and bridle appeared before them huffing and puffing.

It dipped its head up and down and then started off on its way back along the grass track again. "That's my wife's horse!" Lord Hart Williams exclaimed and quickly they followed it down the track towards the East Wood. It wasn't long before Martha's lantern came into view glowing in the distance. And soon Lord Hart Williams was filled with relief as he saw the fair face of his beloved wife in the flickering glow. After their hearty greeting and many thanks to Martha, Lord Hart Williams blew his long brass horn loudly. The others heard it in the distance and followed the call to the old oak. All were relieved when they saw Lady Hart Williams safe and sound. They listened with amazement when they heard what had happened to her that night. Then they all rode wearily back to the village, except for Martha, who stood a while gazing up into the wonder of the night sky.

Later, as the dawn began to break, the owls flew back into their hole in the tree and the pixies lay fast asleep in their little beds somewhere under the roots of the old oak.

Chapter 9

The Garden by the River

One very fine morning in August, the sun rose into a sky that was as blue as blue could ever be! The air was alive with joyful swallows and many butterflies danced around the wild flowers that bloomed beside the road.

Samantha was picking daisies on the village green. Her hair was in plaits and she wore a pretty white scarf around her head. Gabriel soon appeared next to her. They chatted whilst Samantha made herself a daisy-chain necklace.

Gabriel was excited that morning for Sammy and he were to go fishing in the River Mistle. "Can I come too?" Asked Samantha, even though she didn't really like fishing. "Alright," said Gabriel. "I'll ask Dad, but you will have to be very quiet." "I will, I promise," she said as she skipped happily home to ask her mother. Soon the three met by the old elm before they set off down the track towards the marsh.

When they got to the edge of the village, they were greeted by Old Weather John who was sitting on a wooden chair with a cup of tea in his hand. He was watching the busy bees flying in and out of their hive. Whilst Sammy talked to him, Gabriel and Samantha marvelled at the swallows swooping down for flies over the village pond.

The sun felt hot as they walked over the open marshes towards Bramley Wood and, when they entered the wood, they were glad to be under the shade of the overhanging beech leaves. They looked down at the river's deep cool water, swirling through pools and tumbling gently over rocks. The three made their way down the steep bank with rucksack and rod, to find the best place to settle by the water. Sammy remembered a good place with a deep pool and mossy rocks on which to sit nearby. They all dug for worms in the soft woodland earth and before you could say 'Fairy Foxglove' the line was in the water.

Now it wasn't long before Samantha wanted to explore, and so she stood up very quietly and began to climb up the rugged riverbank. She looked back two or three times at Gabriel and Sammy to make sure she was being quiet enough, but just when she got near the top, a stone loosened from under her shoe which rolled down the bank, bounced off a tree and went 'splash' in the water, just where they were fishing! "Oops," said she, then all that could be heard was: "Shhhh, stop it, don't do that!" From Gabriel. "Sorry," whispered Samantha. Gabriel imagined that every fish would have swum all the way down the river to the sea in fright. "Don't worry, they won't do that," reassured Sammy.

Samantha got to the top of the riverbank and there she found a big flat rock. It was like a table covered with a green mossy cloth! She lay on it and looked up at the great branches high above her. Then she closed her eyes and felt the warm summer breeze on her face. A while later she had an idea. She hopped down off the mossy rock and collected many little flat stones, which she put in her apron. Next, she found pieces of tree bark, clumps of moss and some twigs. She climbed back on to the rock putting the treasures from her apron in front of her. Samantha lay down on her tummy. Then, one by one, she made a garden wall out of all the little flat stones. Next, she took a piece of bark, which made a very fine gate. Samantha hummed a little tune softly to herself whilst she worked. "Ahh," she thought, jumping back down off the rock. She returned with some clay in one hand and sand in the other. Pushing the twigs into the clay and dressing the twigs with moss she had made the finest little trees for her garden.

Meanwhile, down by the river, no fish had been caught but they had seen a brown trout leaping for flies. Gabriel was getting bored, so he and Sammy decided to go for a walk. They rested the rod on a forked branch and put a little bell on the end. Now, if they caught a fish, the rod would wobble and the bell would ring.

Samantha watched them from her mossy table high above.

By now, her garden was looking beautiful. She had made a little garden house out of bark and moss. Using the sand, she sprinkled a winding path from the gate up through her garden, and there were flowers each side of the path. With her nimble fingers, Samantha was now making a lovely fairy out of clay, sticks and a mushroom.

As Sammy and Gabriel walked downriver, they saw Samantha up on the rock, so they waved to one another. "We'll be back soon," Sammy called. When they got to the next pool, they found that it had a high cliff on one side and a little gravel beach next to the water on the other. A great big weeping willow tree hung over the pool with long rope-like branches that almost touched the water. Sammy and Gabriel looked at the long trailing branches, and then looked at each other with big smiles! Sammy found a long, hooked stick and, with Gabriel's help, he pulled a trailing willow branch back, which he then held tightly in both hands. Now with a smile on his face he asked Gabriel: "Do you think I could swing to the other side?" "Of course, Dad!" Gabriel said proudly. So, holding tightly to the willow, Sammy ran to the edge and made a big leap. The whole tree shook as it took Sammy's weight. He swung low over the middle of the pool with both of his feet cutting through the water like those of a landing swan, then up he went again to the other side, above the gravel beach. Sammy let go just at the right moment. He landed with both feet at the water's edge. Crunch! Gabriel jumped up and down clapping. Looking very pleased with himself, Sammy said: "Your turn now Gabriel!" Gabriel took the hooked stick and pulled the willow back, just like his dad had done. He stood at the edge and looked at the water below. "It's a long way down," he said. "You'll be alright," called Sammy. "Just run fast and hold on tight."

Gabriel's legs were much shorter than Sammy's of course, but he ran as fast as he could and took a brave leap off the edge. The warm air blew passed his ears as he flew over the river towards Sammy and the gravel beach. His feet were much higher from the water and when he swung up on the other side, Gabriel looked down at Sammy below. He just couldn't let go! It was too far to drop. The branch swung back the other way. Gabriel hoped that he might jump onto the cliff from where he'd started but he didn't swing far enough. He swung towards Sammy again but didn't reach him. Soon he found himself dangling over the deep water in the middle of the pool holding on tighter than ever to the willow branch. "Oh dear!" said Sammy. He couldn't help laughing loudly. "Don't make me laugh now!" Said Gabriel.

Meanwhile, Samantha lay on her tummy playing joyfully in her garden when a lovely 'ting-a-ling-ting-a-ling' sound came from somewhere. She tilted her head to listen. "Could there be real fairies around here?" She thought. She looked to where the sound was coming from. It was down by the river! Then she saw that the end of the rod was bending up and down! 'Ting-a-ling-ting!' It was the bell on the end of the rod. Samantha jumped off the rock and scrambled down the bank as fast as she could, gathering up her long skirt and apron so as not to trip. When she got down to the pool, she just managed to grab hold of the rod before it would have been pulled into the deep water. She held the rod in her left hand and with her right hand she began slowly to reel in a fish. It pulled this way and that way but slowly and surely Samantha managed to reel it out of the water and onto the rocks. Now, just as she did so, who should appear but one very soaking wet Gabriel! "You caught a fish!" he said. "Yes I did!" Said Samantha, proudly. "I don't know who is wetter, you or the fish!" "Me I think," Gabriel said.

Sammy was very pleased that Samantha had caught a fish and saved his rod too. Whilst Gabriel hung all his wet clothes on branches to dry, Samantha went to finish making her fairy garden. She made a little bowl out of clay, filled it with water and climbed carefully up the bank. She placed the bowl by the garden house, then put stones, moss and flowers all around her lovely pond. She made one more fairy, who sat at the edge of the pond looking dreamily into the water. Samantha was so very happy with her fairy garden but she knew that soon it would be time to leave it. There was just one more thing to do. She collected some bird feathers and some very soft moss. With these she made a cosy bed in the garden house so that when the fairies got tired, they could go in and sleep. Soon she heard Sammy's voice calling out: "Samantha, Samantha it's time to go home." "I'm coming," she answered. She took one last look at her garden then closed the gate before joining the others.

Sammy and Gabriel were very happy when Samantha saw them because they had caught two more fish. Now the three made their way back to Bramley across the marsh. The afternoon sun seemed hotter than ever. Weather John's garden was full of bees and butterflies enjoying the flowers, whilst Weather John himself lay in the shade, deep in his afternoon sleep on his lawn.

The three arrived on the village green feeling hot but happy after such a day. It was now time to say goodbye to Samantha and as she walked up the gravel road holding her fish, Gabriel called after her: "Samantha, do you like fishing now?" She turned and said with a smile: "I like it a bit, but I do prefer making fairy gardens."

Later that night, when Samantha was tucked up asleep in her bed, and when the tawny owl flew in the moonlight over the silvery treetops in Bramley Wood, a dormouse put its little paws up on the wall of the fairy garden by the river. The two fairies heard its little feet coming up the garden path. The mouse sat between the fairies by the pond for a while. They all looked at the moonlight on the water. Then, as the moon began to set behind the trees, the dormouse curled up and fell fast asleep in the cosy little house in the garden by the river.

Chapter 10

The Giant Pumpkin

The winds of change had already begun to blow the feeling of autumn to Bramley. Granny Bambridge had harvested many baskets of vegetables and flowers through the summer months. "This was a good summer," she said to herself as she put green tomatoes on her windowsill to ripen.

Later that day, Granny was stirring a pan of steaming raspberries and syrup to jar for the winter, when she gazed out into her garden. "It's about time to harvest the pumpkins," she thought to herself. Granny had a very fine crop of pumpkins but there was one that was bigger than any pumpkin Granny Bambridge had ever seen, and she had seen many! "What are we to do with that one?" She wondered. Then came a little knock at the door. "That'll be Samantha's knock," Granny thought, and it was! "Come in my dear," Granny called. "What a lot of jam, Granny," said Samantha, looking at all the colourful jars with her big eyes. "Want to try some?" And what do you think Samantha said to that?

"Come with me," said Granny after a while, "I've got something to show you." Samantha followed her out to the vegetable garden. "Close your eyes," said Granny, and then she took Samantha by the hand and

led her to the giant pumpkin. "You can look now!" "Oh my goodness!" Samantha exclaimed, "that's so very, very big!" "I gave it a shovel full of Alder's dung," said Granny with a big smile. "Oh I see," said Samantha stroking its huge orange belly. "What are we to do with such a big pumpkin?" Asked Granny. Samantha looked up and thought for a while. "I know," she said, "why don't we make pumpkin soup for everyone in Bramley!" "Now there's a thought," said Granny with a grin.

That evening Granny had a word with Sammy. Then the very next day, Sammy, Isabel and Gabriel appeared at Granny's gate carrying a long saw, a billhook cutter and a huge saucepan. Samantha was already in Granny's kitchen helping to light the stove. They all went into the garden to inspect the giant pumpkin. First, they made a little prayer of thanks for such a wonderful crop, then Sammy took his billhook cutter and with one great chop he severed the pumpkin at the stalk. "We must roll this giant over," he said, "so as we can cut it in half." They all pushed their hands underneath, counted to three, then heaved and the giant pumpkin rolled slowly onto its side. (The Giant Pumpkin pg2 MJF) "That'll do," said Sammy. His big saw had a handle at each end so Sammy took one end and Gabriel took the other and they started to cut. They cut to and fro, to and fro. Isabel, Granny and Samantha stood on the path in the autumn sunshine with baskets in their hands, ready to take the pieces into the kitchen. The pumpkin began to open a little. Then puffing and blowing they cut through the very last bit. The two halves rolled to the ground. "Hurrah!" They all shouted. The sun lit up the golden flesh of the pumpkin and they all stood for a while admiring it. Sammy began to chop out the flesh with his billhook cutter and one after another, twelve baskets full with orange pumpkin flesh were carried to the kitchen. Sammy was careful not to break through the skin so as the two halves could be put back together again, for they wanted to bring the pumpkin to the village green to show the people of Bramley just how big it was.

Isabel stirred the boiling pumpkin pieces whilst Granny went to the garden to fetch parsley, chives and thyme to add to the soup. Later that day, the giant pumpkin shells and two huge pans of steaming hot soup were loaded onto Alder's cart, bound for the village green. The baker had kindly given a dozen loaves of freshly baked bread to add to the feast. News of the soup quickly got around the village as did its delicious smell and soon Granny and Isabel were filling empty bowls for hungry villagers. But where were Gabriel and Samantha? Surely, they would like to have tried the soup too? They were nowhere to be seen. Sammy and Isabel called for them but still they didn't come. "I'm sure they're not far away," said Granny reassuringly. The villagers were all standing around admiring the giant pumpkin and enjoying the soup when, all of a sudden, the two halves of the pumpkin burst open, and two children leaped out with their arms in the air shouting 'boo!' The villagers all jumped back so quickly that the vicar's feet left his shoes and the landlord's false teeth fell 'plop' into his soup! Everyone laughed and cheered. Then many thanks were given by all for such a delicious harvest gift.

The villagers of Bramley then burst into a hearty song:

"We thank you for the sun
And we thank you for the rain.

For all the seeds we planted
That fed us once again."

"We thank you for our hands
And we thank you for our feet.
For all the tools that work the land
Without which we could not eat."

"We thank you for the fire
Which cooks our food so well.
We thank you for our noses
That always love the smell."

"We thank you for all nature
For nothing do we lack.
May we never only take
But always give some back."

The next day, Gabriel and Samantha were sitting on the bench under the old elm tree looking at the giant pumpkin shells and wondering what might become of them. They were so big and round that they must be good for something. Then, all of a sudden, Gabriel had a bright idea. Samantha smiled when he told her. "Come on, let's go!" So, one by one, they heaved the pumpkin halves down the lane to the village pond, where they placed them next to the water. "Are you sure we won't sink?" Asked Samantha nervously. "There's only one way to find out," said Gabriel. He pushed his half into the water and began to get in. Samantha held onto his sleeve as he did so. The water came quite close to the top but it didn't flood in and Gabriel was afloat, so Samantha took courage and got into her half too. Soon, they floated away from the edge, feeling excited but a little frightened too. But then it wasn't long before they realized they had nothing to paddle with! Oh dear, how were they to get back to the shore?

Quite soon, an old man appeared beside the pond. He wore a black hat and carried a basket in his hand. "That's a funny looking pair of ducks," he said with a laughing voice. The children looked over. It was Weather John. He threw two bits of dried bread out for them. "Aren't you hungry?" He asked the strange pumpkin ducks. "Help!" Shouted Samantha from the middle of the pond. "We haven't any paddles!" "Haven't you got paddle feet?" Asked Weather John. The two children began to laugh, but they couldn't laugh too much in case the water came over the sides. Weather John went off to his shed, and then he came back with a length of rope. Holding one end, he threw the rest out to the helpless pumpkin ducks. Soon they were safely back at the edge of the pond. "I wouldn't try that again," said Weather John. "What if I hadn't seen you?" "Thank you for saving us," said the children gratefully to Old Weather John as they turned their pumpkin boats upside down and put them by the bulrushes near the water's edge.

When the first heavy frost came that winter and the ducks slid on the newly formed ice, Weather John had a good idea. He took a sharp knife to the pond and cut two rounded openings in the side of the pumpkin shells. Then he put a bundle of straw inside each one. It wasn't long before the ducks used them as a place to sleep at night. Do you think the ducks may have laid eggs in them in the spring?

But one thing is for sure, the story of Granny Bambridge's giant pumpkin became another one of Bramley's many tales that lived on and on...

Chapter 11

The Seven Great Limes

Late one afternoon in the month of October Sammy was in the wood, cleaning mud from the wheels of his cart. Alder was standing nearby grunting and stamping his feet impatiently. "Wo, wo!" Shouted Sammy. "I'm coming boy, I'm coming!" Alder stamped his feet once more. It was getting dark and the treetops were swaying in the gusting winds. Sammy noticed the clouds racing past the rising moon. "There's a storm coming," he said to Alder, as he lit his lamp and wiped it with a rag. Alder looked at him: "Yes I know, I was trying to tell you," he said without words. By the time they got out of the wood and onto the moor, the cold wind was whistling around Sammy's hat and through Alder's mane, but they just kept going towards the little lights of Bramley Village.

It felt like a long ride home. When they finally got there, Alder trotted eagerly over the meadow to his shelter whilst Sammy ran to his cottage as big drops of rain began to pelt sideways in the wind. He shut the strong wooden door behind him and there to meet him were Isabel and Gabriel's cheerful faces, the smell of roasting parsnips and a warm crackling fire in the hearth. "We thought you might have been blown away Dad," said Gabriel.

That evening they sat together by the fire and listened to the rumbling of the wind in the chimney. Isabel was knitting, Gabriel had fallen asleep and Sammy had his arm inside a cupboard that wouldn't open much because of the big armchair he was sitting in. Inside the cupboard was an untidy pile of books and other old things that his grandfather had left there. Sammy's fingers came upon a thin leather-bound book. He turned it sideways to get it through the door, and then he held it carefully in both hands. It was thick with dust, which he blew into the hearth making Isabel sneeze. "You could have done that with a cloth!" she said. "Mmm," said Sammy as he peered through a magnifying glass at some writing on the first page. "Secrets of Bramley Wood," it read. "I'm sorry about the dust my dear, but this is very interesting," he said to Isabel. As Sammy turned the pages, he saw that it was written in old-fashioned writing with an ink pen. The pages felt like dried leaves. Some were loose and folded at the corners, others had pressed flowers in-between them. Using his magnifying glass, Sammy began to read. The writer was explaining that in the north of Bramley Wood there were seven great lime trees that were taller than any other trees in the wood, and in these trees there lived 'the little people.' They were just the height of a tawny owl and were as thin as twigs, but were strong and brave. They could move as fast as the swift and climb as well as any squirrel. These little people were known as the Tree Elves and they were there to guard the wood from the unruly witch that lived on the wild misty moor to the north, beyond the wood. Sammy wondered if any of them still lived there. As he turned the pages over, he saw drawings of the Tree Elves. Their faces were narrow, with pointy noses, their hair thick and black. Dressed in clothes made from

woven moss and lime leaves, the men all carried a bow and a sheath of arrows on their backs. The women wore finely made lime-leaf skirts dyed dark red with the berry of the elder and laced with little white flowers of stitch-wort. They wore lime flowers in their hair and necklaces made from seed-pods.

Isabel looked over at Sammy who had now fallen asleep with the book on his lap. She put the book back in the cupboard and gently woke him up. "Time to fill the hot water bottles," she whispered.

The next morning, the wind had dropped, the rain had gone and the sun shone on the great flooded moorland between Bramley Village and the wood. There were some broken roof tiles on the track and a branch of the elm tree lay on the village green. "That was quite a storm last night!" Sammy thought to himself as he rode Alder down the lane to the edge of the flooded moor. How beautiful the water looked, sparkling in the sunlight. Sammy could see a great flock of starlings twisting and turning in the sky as he sat on his horseback near the water's edge. The foresters, being wise, had stuck hazel poles in the marsh each side of the track all the way to the wood so as they could find their way across in such flooded times. Alder took Sammy through the flood with the cold water right up to his tummy. What a brave horse he was! In the wood, the river sounded like thunder as it rumbled under the stone bridge, white with bubbles and spinning with whirlpools.

The foresters talked of fallen trees and floods as they held their cups of steaming tea around the hot stove in the forest lodge. "Now," said Jim the head forester, "I have a task for someone who doesn't mind a long ride today." Jim read aloud some measurements from a sheet of paper.

A ship that was being built on the coast needed an unusually big piece of oak for its keel. This could only be found in the north of the wood where the biggest and oldest oaks grew. "I'll go," said Sammy. He loved to explore wild places, so he took the sheet of paper with him and set off with Alder to the north of the wood. With all the swollen streams and fallen branches they had to cross, it took them all of two hours to get there.

The North Wood was a wild place indeed. It was dense with holly and yew trees. Little animal tracks went from one place to another and for every step Alder took, a hundred little creatures would hide. The further north they went, the bigger and older were the oaks, with their heavy twisting limbs reaching out from enormous trunks. The woodland floor was rugged with great boulders of rock and bogs so deep that even the strongest horses would shy away from those. Sammy loved the beauty of this place. He left Alder to graze a lush grassy patch in a shaft of sunlight. Sammy hopped up on a nearby rock and gazed deep into the wood. He noticed seven enormous lime trees some way off that towered high into the sweet forest air. The tallest branches reached higher than any other in the wood. "I must go and see these," Sammy thought to himself, "before I look for the oaks."

He stood before the seven giant limes and cast his eyes up and down the great trunks. In that moment, he remembered his Grandfather's strange book that he'd found in the cupboard next to his armchair. "Ahh," he said to himself, "could this be the home of the Tree Elves?" Sammy sat down on a mossy stone and took a sandwich from his cloth bag. Then, closing his eyes for a moment, he thanked each one of his chickens for the eggs that stuck out of the side of his bread along with chives and watercress.

At that moment, Sammy didn't know that he was being watched by many little eyes from the lime trees. He was being watched by a family of five jackdaws, a handsome jay, a big yellow-eyed raven and nearly one hundred little tree elves who were all very well hidden in the branches. Sammy looked up and down the lime trees carefully many times. Again, he wondered: "Could the elves still be here to this day?" He finished his sandwich, closed his eyes and listened to all the sounds of the North Wood. High above him, he could hear the call of a buzzard and the rushing sound of wind in the treetops. He could hear the fluttering of a wood pigeon in a nearby holly. He could hear the squeaking of mice in a hollow tree-root behind him, and he could hear a family of jackdaws: "wah, wah, wah" around the lime trees. Then, just as Sammy began to doze off, there came the faint sound of whistling. With a start, he opened his eyes. Was that a bird in the lime trees? He could see nothing. He stood up and went a little closer. The whistling had stopped but then, before Sammy could say 'dotted yellow loose strife,' a sharp little arrow came hissing through the air and went straight into the rim of his hat. In great surprise, Sammy whipped his hat off. "My goodness, a tiny arrow!" He exclaimed, holding his hat in both hands. The point was made of sharp flint, the tail of neatly cut pigeon feathers, and the stick of willow. Then a stern voice called out from very nearby: "And who might you be?" Sammy looked down to where the voice came from. There to his astonishment, standing on a fallen branch, was one of the little people he had seen in his Grandfather's book. He was peering at Sammy with one eye shut and the other looking along the shaft of an arrow that he'd pulled back in the tight string of his bow. "I am Sammy, one of the seven foresters of Bramley," said Sammy, rather nervously. "Ahh, I thought you might be," said the Tree Elf, who appeared to look like everything else on the woodland floor, with his moss tunic and lime leaf trousers. Even his beard and hair looked like the fur of a vole. He put the arrow back in its sheath and the bow on his shoulder. "I've heard of you," said the Elf looking at Sammy with bright shiny eyes. "From whom have you heard of me?" Sammy asked. "A certain person from the West Wood," said the Elf. "She goes by the name of Martha." "Martha! Well, I never…!" Exclaimed Sammy. "And not a word did she ever say about the Tree Elves…" He thought to himself. "Is it true," asked Sammy, "that you elven folk protect the wood from the bad witch?" "Yes, that's right," said the Elf, "for we have eyes that can see further than the hills of the moor, and eyes that can see through fog and the very darkness of night." Sammy pondered for a while. "Then what do you do if you see the bad witch coming into Bramley Wood?" "Firstly," said the Elf, "we fire many arrows into the ground around her. If she does not heed our warning then we have no choice. An arrow dipped in one of Martha's special potions is fired into the bad witch's leg. Then the witch can't help but fall into a deep sleep for all of one whole day. Quickly, the messenger raven is called to fly to the West Wood to tell Martha," said the Elf, pointing to a big yellow-eyed raven high up in a lime tree. The Elf continued: "Martha binds the sleeping witch to the back of a great stag and takes her far, far over the hills of the north moor and lays her in a cave. It is there she will stay until she awakens, and hopefully she stays away for a long time after that." Just then there came the strangest sound from the lime trees. It sounded like a flock of birds all whistling at once. "I must go quickly," the Elf said, "It could be that the bad witch is on the moor."

With his breath held, Sammy watched the Elf run across the wet leaves and up that tree he went, as nimble as a squirrel. Now, this time Sammy noticed that the seven lime trees were bristling with many little elves. The women elves were climbing down the bark, disappearing into holes with their young whilst the men, bows and arrows on the ready, were climbing up to the treetops. Sammy had a feeling that he should quickly find Alder and return home. All the birds had stopped singing. Everything went quiet. Sammy's footsteps seemed loud as his big leather boots snapped little twigs on his way. There was Alder in a hollow, shaking his mane and stamping his hooves. Very soon, they were riding the track towards the middle wood. The mist was setting in and it was then that Sammy saw in the distance, running towards the north at full speed, a great majestic stag with Martha on its back. She was clutching its antlers with her hands and both her legs were swung over to one side of its body, her silver red hair flowing behind her. In a flash, she was gone and Sammy knew that the Tree Elves had caught the bad witch that afternoon. Sammy had a big story to tell when he returned home that evening with an arrow in his hat!

Chapter 12

The Bright-Eyed Fox

One cold windy morning in November, the birds were sheltering in the hedges and the people of Bramley went about their work dressed in thick coats and gloves. Smoke blew sideways from the chimneys and leaves were still falling from the oaks in the school playground.

On the side of the grass hill there grew a thicket of hawthorn and brambles. Standing on the edge of the thicket, on a pile of sandy earth, was a bright-eyed fox. The autumn wind was blowing through her beautiful red fur and white-tipped tail. She stretched her body and yawned, for she had just awoken from her cosy bed deep in a hole down under the roots of the brambles. She sniffed the air with her shiny damp nose and looked all around. She was hungry and so were her two cubs under the ground. The bright-eyed fox looked carefully all around her. Then, when she was sure that nobody was about, off she went a-hunting for her breakfast. She trotted through the long grass and down to the hedge at the bottom of the hill. A buzzard was aloft hunting too, so there wasn't a mouse or a rabbit to be seen. She waited patiently for the buzzard to move on but he just kept gliding up and down, up and down above the hill. The longer she waited the hungrier she became. And so did her two cubs.

Just then, her nose caught the smell of something very delicious. So delicious was the smell that she quickly forgot about mice, rabbits and buzzards and found herself following the hedge towards the village. "Stop here," whispered her nose, and so she stopped. Following the scent, she jumped over the flooded ditch and peered through a hole in the thick blackthorn hedge. Now the bright-eyed fox could see exactly why her nose had brought her here. For standing in the middle of the orchard, on the other side of the hedge, was a very fine chicken with its tail up in the air and its beak down in the long golden grass pecking for seeds and grubs. "Oh yes," thought the fox; "there's my breakfast!" But, being a wise and clever fox, she knew that to catch her breakfast she would only have one chance, otherwise she and her two cubs may have to go hungry that day. She crouched down very quietly in the grass and watched the chicken. It took three little steps nearer to the fox. "Good," the fox thought to herself. Then it took two more. Soon it would be time for her to spring out of the bushes and catch the chicken by surprise. What a fine breakfast that would make for her and her hungry cubs on that cold windy morning. She licked her lips, took a deep breath and was about to leap when, all of a sudden, the buzzard swooped down low over the orchard with its eyes on a big grey wood pigeon. The chicken took fright and ran as fast as it could, back through the hole in its pen from where it had got out. "Oh no," thought the fox. Now her breakfast was completely out of sight! The bright-eyed fox waited a long time but there was no sign of the chicken. Well, it could be said that the fox should have given up and gone home, but she was a brave fox and so curious to see

where the chicken had disappeared to. She looked all around and when she was sure that no one could see her, off she went across the orchard. She paused for a bit before she crawled through the hole in the pen.

It just so happened that at that moment, Granny Bambridge was in her kitchen knitting a pair of socks. She was sure that she'd seen something in the corner of her eye, moving toward her chicken pen. "Now if that was a fox..." She said to herself. Granny put down her knitting and tiptoed to her kitchen door. She opened the door with great care and tiptoed over the yard to the chicken pen. Slowly, and silently, she went into the pen. Then, when she peered around the corner into to the nesting box, there was the fox with its bushy tail and its body half in through the open door. Quick as a flash, Granny Bambridge grabbed the fox by the scruff of its neck. "And what do you think you are doing?" She said to the fox, in a very stern voice. They stared at each other for a while, for their eyes were as bright as each others. "So, what am I to do with you Mrs Fox?! I can't have you just walking in here and helping yourself to my chickens for breakfast. That will never do!" Said Granny Bambridge.

Then all of a sudden, there came a sound that sent a big shiver through the fox, and that sound wasn't very far away at all. It was coming from just the other side of the blackthorn hedge! It was the sound of a hunter's horn! Granny Bambridge turned her head just in time to see 20 or 30 hunting dogs all running through the hole in the hedge. They were sniffing the scent of the fox and were following it to the chicken pen. The dogs soon surrounded the pen, all howling and barking they were. Granny Bambridge made a quick decision. She put the fox in the nesting house with the chickens and shut the door properly. The fox ran into the corner, folded up its legs and put its chin on the ground with the tail over its eyes. She was shaking all over.

Granny Bambridge looked at the dogs. "Shoo, shoo, go away!" She shouted. But the dogs just carried on howling and barking. Then she spotted the hole in the pen, so quickly she mended it to stop the dogs getting in. And, as she was doing so, a huge black horse jumped right over the top of the hedge. The rider was dressed in a bright red jacket and a black velvet hat. "And what do you think you and your dogs are doing here?" Asked Granny Bambridge in a very stern voice. "We are looking for the fox," said the hunter. "Well, you won't find a fox here so you may as well go," said Granny. "But look," said the hunter, "my dogs have followed the scent of the fox right here to your chicken house." "Well then, I think your dogs must be lost," said Granny. "But, if my dogs would kill the fox, then the fox wouldn't eat your chickens," said the hunter. "And if the fox would eat the rabbits, then the rabbits wouldn't eat your vegetables," said Granny. The hunter whistled to the dogs and they all disappeared from Granny Bambridge's orchard, never to be seen there again.

Granny went into the chicken house to see if all was well. Could it be that the fox had eaten the chickens whilst Granny had seen off the hunter? When Granny opened the door of the nesting box, there lay the bright-eyed fox on the floor with the chickens high up on the perch above it. "There," said Granny with a smile, "we're all still here." "Go on home now," Granny said to the fox, clapping her hands. Then the bright-eyed fox ran out of the door, across the orchard and disappeared through the hole in the blackthorn hedge, the white tip of her tail being the last Granny saw of her.

Later that night, Granny wandered up the hill with a hurricane lamp in one hand and a big bag of delicious kitchen scraps in the other. She placed the scraps on the pile of fresh earth as she did many a time in the cold months of that winter. The fox could smell Granny's scent on the food and, do you know, Granny Bambridge never did lose any of her chickens to the bright-eyed fox.

Chapter 13

Midwinter Story

It was the 21st of December, just a few days before Christmas. Sammy, Isabel and Gabriel put on their mittens that had been hanging on the mantelpiece to warm by the fire. They wrapped up well that morning for the mild wind had swung easterly overnight, turning mist to frost, and puddles to ice. Sammy prepared Alder and the cart, whilst Isabel and Gabriel brought in armfuls of dry firewood from the little barn in the garden.

They then set off, as they did every year on that day, to fetch a Christmas tree from Bramley Wood. As the cart rounded the windy corner, they pulled their hats down over their ears, before Old Weather John's cottage came into view. They stopped by the village pond where Weather John was throwing scraps out for the hungry ducks that were all running and sliding on the ice as they chased after the dried bread and vegetable peelings. The four watched with great amusement.

"Today is a special day," said Weather John as he paused for a while and turned his head to the pale sun, which had just risen in the east. "Today is the shortest day of the year," he said, "for it is the winter solstice, and soon a new year will be born." They all stopped and looked at the sun's golden glow, lighting up the treetops of Bramley Wood in the distance. A big flock of starlings flew across the moor and the world would have been quite silent but for the ducks squabbling over their breakfast! Weather John took a few steps closer and looked at the three. "Snow will come by nightfall," he said. "It may stay on the ground at least till Yuletide, heavy snow too!" Isabel looked into Weather John's brown eyes. "How can you tell?" She asked. "Well earlier this morning," he explained, "I sat next to my fire warming my hands and whilst waiting for the kettle to boil, I put on a big damp log. Then a while later, that log started to steam, whistle and hiss. It was making all sorts of funny noises! I was just thinking it was time to let the chickens out when I thought I heard the log say something!" "Really!" Exclaimed Isabel. "Yes, it said my name. Then this is what it said, if I remember rightly:"

"John of the Weather
Now listen to me.
Just for one moment
Before you have tea."

"This morning it's cold
All misty and still.
Not even a breeze
For to turn the windmill."

"But tonight it will change
For to say the least.

The cold wind will rise
And blow hard from the east."

"The tree tops will bend
And the owl it will hide.
Then the snow will come down
Between now and Yuletide."

"So John of the Weather
Take a warning from me.
For tonight it will snow
Yes tomorrow you'll see."

"All that's around you
Will change tonight.
For tomorrow the world will be
Silent and white."

"Tell all whom you meet
Tell all who come past.
To go with good steed
This fine weather won't last."

They all looked at one another. Even the ducks went quiet. The last few starlings flew past. Gabriel was becoming filled with excitement. How wonderful! Feeding the ducks, getting the tree, the shortest day, the starlings, Christmas is coming and so is snow! It was all too much! Gabriel shrieked with excitement and did a little dance on a frozen puddle. Everyone laughed out loud. Then they thanked Old Weather John for his warning. Soon it was time to continue on their way towards the wood and for Weather John to go back to his warm fire.

As they crossed the old stone bridge in the wood, who should they see walking slowly beside the river, but Old Roland. He carried a small Christmas tree on his shoulder and was very grateful when offered a ride on the cart back to his cottage. As they climbed the hill through the hazel wood, Alder pulled hard on the shafts. They rode high over the river cave and down through the ancient holly wood on the other side of the hill. Gabriel looked up at Old Roland's weathered face. He had dewdrops on the ends of his bushy eyebrows. Roland looked back at Gabriel with a smile. "You know what they say," said Roland in his tuneful voice, "they say that this is the very road that Father Christmas takes when he rides through the wood on his way to Bramley. And these are the very holly trees from where he collects the red-berry-covered branches." Gabriel looked up at the crown of the trees. They were laden with berries glowing bright in the misty sun that was now as high as it could be on that shortest day of the year. "Has anyone ever seen him?" Gabriel asked. "Only the gnome folk," said Roland. "Sometimes they help him cut the ivy and provide hazel nuts to take to the village." You see, in those days, in those faraway places in the west, Father Christmas was dressed in green. He was as green as the leaves of the holly, so even the gnomes had to look hard to see him.

They rode down the winding track and arrived at the gate of Old Roland's cottage. He invited them in whilst Alder had a good drink from the river and filled his tummy with grass from the bank. Roland served hot apple juice and told them a wonderful midwinter tale. Gabriel, Isabel and Sammy carried many logs to the cottage for the coming of the snow. Roland was very thankful. They bid him a hearty farewell and started off along the track to the West Wood.

The air was getting colder and the wind was now turning gusty from the east. They rode past an enormous old oak tree that was still clinging to some of its leaves. Its trunk was as wide as the cart, and its high twisty branches almost disappeared into the mist. Isabel sang a song as they rode deeper into the hazel wood but then they could hear another voice singing along too! It was coming from nearby. Who could it be? They kept riding, but the voice seemed to follow them. Then they could hear the sound of footsteps crunching in the leaves and the snapping of twigs. Sammy pulled on the reins. "Woah boy!" Alder dug his hooves into the frosty mud and the cart came to a halt near a big chestnut tree. The song was coming from there somewhere. Isabel sang as she jumped off the cart. She went around the tree and when she appeared again, who should be with her, arm in arm?

It was Martha! Martha had been out collecting mistletoe from the old oak. There they stood singing the last chorus loudly:

"Oh, we'll all dress in green
And we'll all dress in white.

Then we'll cut the merry mistletoe
And bind it up so tight."

"Tour-a-lu-la-lu-la-lee
Tour-a-lu-la-lu-la-ley."

"And we'll sing a merry tune
On a mid-winter's day."

They all laughed together.

Martha carried a stout branch of hazel in her hand, and from the branch there hung several bunches of mistletoe covered with misty white berries. Martha greeted them with merry midwinter wishes and a kiss on the cheek. "Would you like to come to my cottage for hot pear juice and scones?" "Oh yes please." said Gabriel. They all rode down the long hill to Martha's cottage. How beautiful it looked with its straw roof and jolly yellow jasmine flowers around the door to welcome winter visitors. Martha's cottage always smelt so sweetly of herbs, a little hazel wood smoke and, on that day, wild plum jam. Martha soon put the scones, plum jam and hot pear juice on the little round table in front of the hearth. The fire crackled merrily. They talked and laughed whilst Rosie the cat lay fast asleep on Isabel's lap. Martha asked Gabriel: "Have you got your sledge ready for the snow?" Gabriel mouth was so full of scones and jam that all he could do was nod. Sammy peered out of the window. "The light is fading," he said. "We'd better go and find our tree before it gets too dark." They thanked Martha heartily and set off once again towards the North Wood. It wasn't long before the clouds began to gather and it seemed to get quite dark as they rode through a pinewood along a very bumpy track. They soon got to the place where Sammy thought they would find a good tree for their cottage. Whilst the others wandered among the trees, Alder tucked in to a nice sack of oats. They all saw the right tree at the same time. It was as tall as Sammy, thick and round. Little chips of wood fell to the ground as Sammy cut the trunk with his small axe.

Isabel and Gabriel held on to the tree on their ride through Bramley Wood, and down onto the frozen marshes below. The east wind chilled their faces as the last of the midwinter sun sank through the fingers of the trees and into the arms of the wood like a smouldering log.

Sammy lit the two hurricane lamps that hung on the front of the cart. They saw the first flakes of snow fluttering through the flickering light. Alder trotted across the marsh and up the hill to the village. Weather John was happy to see them go by from his armchair by the fire. They all slept soundly that night wrapped in their goose-feather quilts. But outside, the east wind blew and it blew all night long. Then, as the new dawn broke, two little hands wiped the ice off the window with the help of warm breath and when Gabriel could see out, to his joy, the world was covered with deep glistening white snow.

That morning, after breakfast, every child in Bramley could be seen making snowmen and sledging down the hill. More snow fell the next day, and it was time to prepare for Christmas. Granny Bambridge's pies could be smelled in the road as she rolled more pastry on the table by her hot oven. Isabel unwrapped her Christmas pudding that she had made with fruits and spices weeks before.

On Christmas Eve, the sky was filled with twinkling stars. Across the smooth white moor, Bramley Wood shone silently in the moonlight. Every twig and branch hung heavily with snow. The birds were huddled together sleeping in the shelter of hollow trees and snow-covered blackthorn. The only one who was about in the wood on that frosty silent night wore deerskin booths. He was walking towards the hill of holly. He had come from somewhere deep in the woods perhaps.

All the people of Bramley Village by now had bathed in their metal tubs next to their fires and were putting on their very best clothes for to go to church. (Midwinter Story pg6 MJF)

Isabel brushed her long hair by the mirror before tying it up. She wore a long dress of dark purple, edged with lace. Around her waist was a plum-coloured band of silk, and on her shoulders she wore a poppy-red shawl. Lastly, she put on her pretty hat with feathers on the front. Sammy wore his best leather booths, a fine black jacket with waistcoat and trousers and a dark green neck scarf. Gabriel wore the same except that his jacket was green and his neck scarf was red. The people of Bramley looked so fine as they walked in the light of the moon through the village towards the church. The frozen snow crunching under their feet filled Gabriel with delight. The path to the church was lit up with little lanterns on either side, as was every grave in the churchyard. All were greeted at the door by Father Appleby. The church looked beautiful, glowing with candles and decorated with holly and ivy boughs. Hymns and carols were sung, and then the children sang sweetly in the choir. The villagers bid one another a peaceful Christmas as they made their way home to feast.

Later that night, when all were fast asleep, Gabriel awoke to a strange sound outside. What could it be? The cold east wind gusted around the roof of the cottage, but it wasn't that he heard, no! Gabriel thought he could hear something else. It sounded like little bells jangling in the distance. He sat up to look out of the window, but it was covered with little patterns of frost. Gabriel tried breathing on the glass but could only see out a little before it froze over again. The sound got nearer. Gabriel couldn't tell whether the sound came from below or above. "I'm sure it's bells," he thought in puzzlement. Then it stopped and at that moment there was a crunching sound like many hooves. "How very odd," he thought. Quite a lot of snow fell past the little frozen window as it slid down off the roof. Gabriel thought he heard a strange thumping noise coming from inside the chimney. Now the wind was howling around the cottage. A little soot fell into the fireplace. Gabriel's shoulders were feeling cold so he got back into his bed, wrapping his arms around his hot water bottle. Then, was it the bells he heard once more, before they faded away in the distance? And he was sure he saw little golden lights high above the roof! Before he could wonder any more, Gabriel slipped gently back into his dreams....

When he awoke, it was Christmas Day! The sun shone, shimmering through his window, lighting up the beautiful frost patterns, all silver, blue and golden. Gabriel smiled to himself and then he noticed a stocking hanging on the end of his bed, tied at the top with ivy. Excitedly, he took the stocking, and down the stairs he ran. He was greeted by his mother and father who were setting the table for breakfast. "Aa ha!" said Sammy looking at Gabriel's stocking. "I see that Father Christmas has been!" Flames were dancing over the oak logs in the hearth. Gabriel spoke excitedly during breakfast. He spoke of the bells, the strange noises in the chimney and the golden lights he saw in the night. Soon there was a knock, knock, knock and Gabriel ran to the door. It was Granny Bambridge and Old Weather John. They all lovingly sat around the fire, opening presents and thanking God for giving them life. They sang songs and told stories all day long.

Alder stood quietly in his stable and the low rays of the winter sun were just enough to warm his cream and brown dappled coat. He was so happy to see Sammy coming across the bright snowy meadow with a big bucket of crunchy Christmas carrots.

And so ended another good year in Bramley, where the people and nature worked as one.

The End

CPSIA information can be obtained
at www.ICGtesting.com
Printed in the USA
LVHW060108260722
724372LV00011B/303